Willy and the Cardboard Boxes

WILLY
and the Cardboard Boxes

LIZI BOYD

VIKING

For Pop and Nicholas

VIKING
Published by the Penguin Group
Viking Penguin, a division of Penguin Books USA Inc.,
375 Hudson Street, New York, New York 10014, U.S.A.
Penguin Books Ltd, 27 Wrights Lane, London W8 5TZ, England
Penguin Books Australia Ltd, Ringwood, Victoria, Australia
Penguin Books Canada Ltd, 2801 John Street, Markham, Ontario, Canada L3R 1B4
Penguin Books (N.Z.) Ltd, 182–190 Wairau Road, Auckland 10, New Zealand

Penguin Books Ltd, Registered Offices: Harmondsworth, Middlesex, England

First published in 1991 by Viking Penguin, a division of Penguin Books USA Inc.

1   3   5   7   9   10   8   6   4   2

Copyright © Lizi Boyd, 1991   All rights reserved

Library of Congress Cataloging in Publication Data
Boyd, Lizi, 1953-
Willy and the cardboard boxes / Lizi Boyd.   p.   cm.
Summary: With the help of his imagination and a lot of empty boxes
at his father's office, Willy flies into a colorful world where the
boxes become a boat, horse, fire truck, and more.
I S B N   0 - 6 7 0 - 8 3 6 3 6 - 2
[1. Boxes—Fiction.   2. Imagination—Fiction.
3. Play—Fiction.]   I. Title.
PZ7.B6924Wi   1991   [E]—dc20   90-24920   CIP   AC

Printed in Hong Kong   Set in 16 point Egyptienne 505

"Today you can go to work with me," said Willy's dad.

"All right!" said Willy.

Willy likes to ride the bus to his dad's office.

He can see buildings, trucks, cars, and even an
airplane from his seat on the bus.

New computers have just arrived at the office.

Willy and his dad help unpack the boxes.

"You can play with these boxes," said Willy's dad.

He gives Willy markers, scissors, and string.

Willy decides to build an airplane. He flies up

in the air over his dad's desk. He waves good-bye.

Willy flies over fields and mountains.

He lands on a little island.

Willy wants to go fishing so he builds himself a rowboat.

Across the water, Willy sees a forest.

He builds a tunnel and walks through.

When he climbs out, Willy is surrounded by high fences.

Willy knows a horse could jump those fences.

He makes a horse and gallops off. Willy's horse begins
to whinny. He smells smoke and so does Willy.

Willy hops off his horse and builds a fire engine.

He rings the bell and sounds the siren.

Willy sees a barn that's in flames.

He sprays his hose and puts out the fire.

Suddenly Willy feels very hungry.

He builds a car and goes speeding off.

He drives back to the city for lunch.

Willy builds an elevator and walks in.

He presses a button that takes him to the top of a building.

Willy opens up the doors and makes a restaurant.

There are lots of people in the restaurant.

Everyone sits down to eat their lunch.

Then Willy builds a train.

He rides by all the buildings, up over a high bridge,
and off toward the countryside again.

Willy comes to a field and builds a circus ring.

He fills the seats with people and
makes a baby elephant and a trick dog.

Willy stays at the circus for a long, long time.

He sees lots of different animals.

But Willy is getting tired.

Willy builds himself a house.

He curls up and falls asleep.

"It's time to go home, Willy," says his dad, peeking in
the door of Willy's house. "Already?" asks Willy.

Willy and his dad get back on the bus.

The trick dog rides home with them, too.